ALLAN AHLBERG

Slow Dog Falling

Illustrated by
ANDRÉ AMSTUTZ

VIKING • PUFFIN

VIKING/PUFFIN
Published by the Penguin Group: London, New York, Australia, Canada and New Zealand
Penguin Books Ltd, Registered Offices: Harmondsworth, Middlesex, England

First published by Viking 1999
1 3 5 7 9 10 8 6 4 2
Published in Puffin Books 1999
1 3 5 7 9 10 8 6 4 2

Printed in Hong Kong by Imago Publishing Ltd

A CIP catalogue record for this book is available from the British Library
ISBN 0–670–87992–4 Hardback
ISBN 0–140–56398–9 Paperback

Slow Dog is thinking,
"I . . . think . . . I . . . will
pick some apples."

Slow Dog picks some apples.
The chickens come running by.

Fast Fox comes running by.
Slow Dog . . . falls.

The next day
Slow Dog is thinking,
"I . . . think . . . I . . . will
clean the windows."

Slow Dog cleans the windows.
The chickens come running by.

Fast Fox comes running by.
Slow Dog . . . falls.

The *next* day
Fast Fox is thinking,
"I think I will
tie Slow Dog up."

Fast Fox ties
Slow Dog up.

The chickens come running by.
"I think I will catch those chickens,"
Fast Fox thinks.

"And take them home," he thinks.

"And make a chicken stew!"

Time goes by.
Mother Hen is thinking,
"Where are those chickens?"

Slow Dog is thinking,
"I . . . think . . . I . . . am
all tied up."

Fast Fox is thinking,
"Stew!"

Mother Hen looks for the chickens,

and looks . . . and looks.

A little house in the woods.
Cheep, cheep, cheep!
A little smoke from the chimney.
Cheep, cheep, cheep!
A little light at the window.
Cheep, cheep, cheep!
A little chicken . . .

...in a pot!

Fast Fox is reading his cookbook.
Potatoes – yes!
Peas and carrots – yes, yes!
Salt and pepper and dark brown gravy
yes, yes, yes!
And chicken – YES!

And chicken – NO!

Mother Hen rushes in
and grabs the chickens –

cheep, cheep, cheep! –
and rushes out.

Time flies.
Mother Hen and the chickens
run back through the woods.
Fast Fox is close behind.

Mother Hen is thinking,
"My poor little chickens!"
Fast Fox is thinking,
"My lovely stew!"

Slow Dog is thinking,
"I . . . think . . ."
The chickens come running by.
" . . . I . . . am . . ."
Mother Hen comes running by.
" . . . nearly . . ."
Fast Fox comes running by.

"...*untied!*"

Slow Dog . . .

falls.

The End

THE FAST FOX, SLOW DOG BOOKS

Did you enjoy this story?
Would you like to read another?
Try

The Hen House

It is bedtime in the Hen House –
tiptoe, tiptoe –
and somebody is creeping up
and creeping in
and grabbing the chickens!

Oh no! Those poor chickens . . .

. . . who can save them?